SNAKE SNACK

COCKY COBRAS BOOK 2

TILLY POPE

ABOUT SNAKE SNACK

The life of a cobra shifter isn't easy.
Thanks Mom and Dad for that bombshell.

Aidan
I love working with cars...and my brothers.
The smell of grease and oil...heaven to me.
I thought my life was set up perfectly.
A new home with a loving girlfriend.
Or so I thought...until *she cheated on me.*
Now I'm heartbroken...and grumpy as hell. I never thought I'd find love again.
But a chance meeting at the store changes everything.
A beautiful woman. Perfect for me in every way.
I'm scared she'll freak out when she finds out what I truly am.
But the snake in my pants wants to escape.
And claim her for my own.

Short, hot, and over the top! If you love possessive alpha males, totally unrealistic insta-love romance, this one's for you! No cliffhanger, no cheating, and a guaranteed HEA!

For all my super yummy over the top readers!
Who's your daddy?

1

*A*idan
    I'm genuinely happy for my brother. Connor deserves a girl like Alana in his life. She's a wonderful girl. Good for him.

Yet I can't help feeling a sickening seed of jealousy bury itself in my gut as I lean against the Toyota I'm supposed to be working on. I'm watching my brother and his girl nuzzle together and make kissy, lovesick faces to each other. Alana is getting ready to leave to attend a conference for a few days, and neither of them can bear to be apart.

I shouldn't be so bitter, I mean, he's my brother. But I have Allison to thank for that.

Allison fucking Harley. Even all these months later, the mere mention of her name makes my gut coil. That crazy bitch turned my entire life upside down. And it still pisses me off.

It would have been different if she'd just ended our relationship. But she didn't. I'd walked into the house we'd just rented, and she was on the brand-new sofa we'd bought fucking her ex-boyfriend.

Who does that? A slimy skank, that's who.

The worst part about it all is that the no-longer-ex, Tommy, used to be a friend of mine. We went to the same school years ago, hung out at the same gym, and he even introduced me to Allison, saying she was his ex, but they were 'totally over. Just good friends now, is all.'

What a fucking liar. I bet they were seeing each other the whole time Ally and I were a couple. Three years of my life wasted on that woman.

I look over at Connor and Alana as they giggle at each other and wonder if I'll ever have what they have. I mean, I'm happy for *them*, but after Ally and her bullshit, I just want to be left alone.

That's easier said than done. I'm surrounded by people, day in and day out. At the shop, there are always customers, my brothers, and the interns we hired last month. They're all nice guys, but they're young and haven't had their entire lives trampled, yet. They're hopeful, happy, and spend a lot of their time at work laughing and joking with each other. I hate it.

At home, Dara and Brodie are around, but Dara spends most of his time in the garage, or in his small repair shop now that Connor's moved out and taken all his bikes with him. And Brodie spends a lot of time in his room, reading car magazines and listening to podcasts.

Brodie suggested I take a week off and go on vacation somewhere. However, when that vacation is over, I'll have to return home, and all those horrible feelings that go along with it are enough to ruin whatever break I might plan for myself. I'm much better off just staying where I am.

"Aidan!"

I turn to see Dara walking toward me with a piece of paper in his hand. His blond hair is all messed up from where he's been running his hands through it, which he does whenever he's trying to solve a problem. There must be something back in his shop that's giving him trouble.

"What's up?" I ask as he approaches.

"Here's the grocery list. I know it's my turn to go, but I have to finish this Chromebook and get it back to the high school by tomorrow morning. And before you ask, Brodie's staying late to work on that old VW. The engine's still overheating," he says, and hands me the list.

Ugh. I hate grocery shopping. Don't get me wrong. I love food, and I love cooking. I cook most nights for all of us. It's one activity I enjoy, along with reading, but I hate shopping. That involves people, and many of them move at glacial speeds as they look at every chip brand in the aisle. I wish Pythos would get online ordering like every other city in the country, but until it does, every few weeks I drag myself to the local grocery store and stock up.

"You're lucky. It's a brief list this week. Twenty

minutes, tops. If you cut out early, you can beat the rush," Dara says, looking at me with a knowing grin.

All of us McKinley men have introverted tendencies, but Dara and I are the quietest, by far. He prefers to spend his time tinkering with technology, and I prefer to spend mine alone with books or a frying pan. He understands better than anyone about my hesitance to go into a public place filled with a ton of people.

I check my watch. It's 4:15 PM, and If I leave now, I can get to the store and back before the after work rush. Nodding my head, I fold the list and tuck it into the pocket of my jeans.

"Fine. Tell Connor and Brodie I'm leaving. I'll see you at home," I tell Dara.

"Steak quesadillas tonight?" Dara asks.

"You know it!" I say and walk out.

Every Sunday night, my brothers and I sit down to figure out what we want to eat for the upcoming week. Our decision factors in whatever we have in the fridge and pantry, any cravings we have, and whatever's on sale.

This week's menu includes fire-roasted shrimp and pasta, steak and mashed potatoes, and beef lasagna. Quesadillas are our favorite though, because our mom used to make them every Thursday night when we were growing up. It's a tradition I've tried to uphold after Mom and Dad passed away.

She tried to teach us all to cook when we were kids. It was a life skill, she'd said, just like pitching a tent, or changing a tire. Our parents wanted to arm us with as many of these skills as possible, so we could stand on our own two feet as adults.

But while my brothers had paid little attention to Mom and can barely boil an egg, I'd really gotten into the art of cooking.

In fact, the day our parents died, I was baking a cake for them. A welcome home gift using Mom's favorite Guinness chocolate cake recipe from the recipe binder she'd given me. In it is every single recipe we'd ever made together, along with those she'd been handed down by her own mother and grandmother.

The day after their funeral, I opened the binder to the steak quesadilla recipe, and I've been making it every Thursday since. Layering three kinds of cheese and steak between tortillas and heating them in the cast iron skillet that's been a part of our family's kitchen for as long as I can remember.

The quesadillas are pure comfort food that reminds us of the good times, sitting around the table as a family, laughing and enjoying each other's company before everything went to shit.

The good times before Mom and Dad died. Before we became snakes, and life got so complicated.

2

*C*olleen
Two more hours, and then my shift is over. Two more hours, and I can go home and work on my food blog and forget this day ever happened.

It started out fine. Dara over at the McKinley brother's garage fixed my old, broken coffeemaker, so I woke to the wonderful aroma of freshly brewed java this morning. I've been a week without it, and it's been absolute torture having to buy coffee every day.

So, I drank my coffee, went to yoga, and got to work just before nine o'clock. I waved hello to all the familiar faces in the grocery store as I made my way back to the meat department where I spend forty-five hours each week.

The morning tasks and to-dos went by so quickly and I was on a roll. I filled order after order, then my boss, Iona, walked in. She's worked at four grocery store meat departments, and that's after a fifteen-year stint at a fancy real life butcher in Brooklyn, New York.

Why she moved out to the desert, I'll never know. I'd take New York over Pythos in a heartbeat, but the cost of living is so much cheaper here, and I don't have to pay any rent since my grandma left me her house, but still, if I had my way, I'd go NYC all the way.

When Iona walks into the back where we butcher the meat, my hackles immediately go up. She intimidates me. She's so knowledgeable; so experienced, and her resting bitch face would scare the strongest of men. I live in eternal fear of fucking up in her presence.

One time, she caught a new guy throwing away a bunch of chicken livers, and the ass-chewing she gave him was off the chart. He quit a day later, and no one has filled his spot so far. It's just me, Petey, and Robert; two butchers who used to run a shop down the road before the land got bought out to build a Walmart.

"Colleen," Iona says, in her deep Bronx accent which hasn't gotten watered down one bit by all her time spent out west. It also makes her sound scary, which helps her with the whole intimidating employees thing. No one talks back to a woman who sounds like a gangster.

"Hi, Iona! What's up?" I ask as I continue breaking down a large rack of ribs. My hair is netted, my hands are covered in regulation plastic gloves, my apron is as clean as it can get when you work around blood all day long, and I'm dressed in my uniform of chef's pants, a chef's coat, and Crocs. It's the ugliest shoe known to man, but also the most comfortable when you're on your feet for nine hours a day.

"Do you recall our meeting last week?" she asks, folding her arms over her chest and leaning against one of the refrigerators next to my workstation.

"Of course. I took notes. They're in my folder. I can get to it as soon as I..." I trail off, nodding at the giant cleaver in my hand and the ribs resting on the worktop.

"Tell me, did you note down that we were changing our meat delivery schedule at the meeting?" she asks.

I nod as I continue slicing into the ribs, leaving an equal amount of meat on each side of the cut. I know she's a stickler about that kind of stuff.

"Of course. The meat delivery schedule is changing since we finally got a contract with that organic farm in Rancho Cresco. They're delivering every day at 6 a.m., so we're rotating our shifts to accommodate the time slot," I say.

"Yes. And who was supposed to rotate her shift this morning to meet them?" Iona asks.

Oh, crap! Now, I realize what's going on. Why she's glaring at me, like she wants to pick the cleaver up out of my hand and whack me with the handle. *I* was supposed to meet the supplier this morning. *I* was the first person on the new schedule; a position I'd volunteered for.

This, of course, was back when my coffeemaker was working.

"Oh, my gosh. Iona, I am so sorry. There is no excuse. I...I can't believe I messed up like this. Please allow me to

make it up to you and the rest of the team," I say, trying
to keep the hint of desperation out of my voice, though I
suspect I'm unsuccessful.

Iona is staring at me with a mixture of pity and
disdain, which honestly is not that far off from her
normal bitch face, but there's a slight sneer to her lips
that makes me want to curl into a ball and hide in the
walk-in freezer where it's safe, cold, and quiet.

"You're right. There is no excuse. So, you'll take the
early morning shifts for the next three weeks. You'll also
be training the new interns next week. There's three of
them. All high schoolers. Good luck," she says, then
dismisses me with a wave as she walks out, allowing me
to bask in my own freak-out.

There is no way I will be able to get everything done
if I have to work the early shifts for the next three weeks.
I'll have to give up something. And I can't give up my
food blog or the cookbook I'm working on, since they go
hand-in-hand, so I guess I'm giving up sleep. Wonderful
thing my coffeemaker works again. Lord knows, I will
need it.

After I finish breaking down the rack of ribs, I wash
my hands and go up to the counter where a couple of
people are waiting. Robert and I usually switch between
butchering and counter duty throughout the day.
However, since they called him in to meet the meat
supplier so early this morning, he's already gone home.

Thankfully, the rush of folks getting off work and
rushing to get their grocery shopping done hasn't begun,

so I only have these two to serve and they are the best kind of customers—clear, concise, polite. Things are looking up, and then *he* walks in.

I've seen this guy around the store before. He's always in a black t-shirt and jeans with heavy work boots on his feet. His hair isn't quite blonde or brown but isn't red either. Bronze, maybe?

His skin is both freckled and tanned, his arms corded with muscles, with veins that stand out against the hair on his arms.

Yes, I've noticed his arm hair. Truth be told, I spend a lot of time staring at this guy every time he comes in. But I've never served him. He only comes in once every few weeks, and it's always been Robert.

But today is my chance. Today, I'm staying out front here for the rest of my shift, and I know for a fact that Mr. Mystery Man always comes to the meat counter on his grocery trips. He needs protein to feed those lovely muscles of his, after all.

Sure enough, not five minutes after I see him walk into the store, he makes a beeline to the counter with a look of deep contemplation on his face. He's holding a basket in one hand, and a crumpled, hand-written grocery list in the other.

3

*A*idan

Since Ally and I broke up, I've barely looked at another woman. My brothers have suggested I get on one of those dating apps, but that's not how I work. I don't date girls I can't see a future with, and I can't think about dating anyone right now. Or at least, I couldn't until five seconds ago. But as soon as my eyes land on the hottie at the meat counter, my dick twitches and my palms get a little sweaty. I've been numb and cold for months now, but one look at this girl's face has me alive with feeling and a warmth I haven't felt in a long time.

She's wearing a hairnet, but I can still see a mass of golden curls. Her figure is hidden by the large apron she has on, but I can see her face and neck perfectly, and I like what I see. Round face, full lips, and beautiful green eyes framed by dark lashes. Even though she's just staring into space, there's a hint of contemplation in her gaze, like her mind is working on something.

I have to say hello to her. I need steak for the quesadillas, anyway. Damn, how have I not noticed her before? I really need to get to the meat counter more often.

"Hi there. How can I help you?" she asks as I approach. Her voice is very feminine. Kind of sexy.

"Sure. Can I get a pound and a half of New York strip?" I ask, breaking away from her eyes. I scan the trays of meat on sale and see some Andouille sausage. Gumbo sounds great about now and if I order it, I get to stand here looking at her for a few more seconds.

"And...can I also get some of that Andouille sausage over there? Three pounds, please."

"Sure thing," she says brightly, adjusting her gloves before bending over to select what I've ordered. The air is thick between us as she first weighs the steak, and then the sausage. I'm in awkward silence territory when I finally pluck up the courage to speak again.

"I'm....uh, I'm thinking of making a gumbo with the sausage. Do you think I could use frozen shrimp with that?" I know my gumbo, but just talking to her makes me giddy. Maybe I'll ask a few more stupid questions.

"Is the frozen shrimp peeled?" she asks, setting the wrapped pieces of meat down on the counter.

"Nope. Got it from here a couple of months ago to make some shrimp scampi. Didn't use all of it so I froze it that night."

"Oh, then it should be fine. Just defrost it in the fridge, then peel the shells and use them like you normally would for the broth. Should be fine," she tells me as she hands over the bundles of steak and sausage.

"Okay, good," I say, nodding my head. I'm trying to think of something more to say so I can stay here and talk to her a little longer.

"Anything else I can get ya?" she asks, and I swear there's a hint of hope in her voice, like maybe she wants me to stay as well. Like, maybe she's feeling a connection too.

"Uh," I say, wracking my brain for something else to talk about, anything to keep me here.

I take a deep breath, and there's so much anxious energy filling up inside me I must be visibly vibrating. "Look," I say, shoving the grocery list in my pocket and running my hand through my hair. "Colleen," reading her name off the tag affixed to her apron. "You're nice... and pretty... and seem to know a lot about food. This might seem forward, considering we don't know each other, but would you...would you like to go out with me sometime? Coffee? Dinner maybe?"

I exhale deeply, hoping I didn't speak so quickly that she didn't understand what I'd said, because there's no way I can repeat that.

And then she says, "Sure. I'd like that."

"Great," I say, nodding my head and allowing my smile to grow to a socially acceptable width, but not so wide that I start to resemble The Joker. "Can I get your number and call you later?"

She nods and takes off her gloves. She draws out a pen and notebook from her pocket, rips out a clean sheet of paper and writes her number on it.

"I don't get off for another hour, so if you text and I don't answer, it's because my phone is in my locker. It won't be because I don't want to talk to you, because I do," she says.

I smile, glad that I'm not the only one struggling not to lose my cool.

"That's fine. I have some more shopping to do anyway, so I'll text you after dinner," I say.

"What're you going to have?" she asks, brightening up.

"Steak quesadillas."

"Yum! Sounds good," she says.

"Yeah, they are," I answer. "So, talk to you soon?"

"Looking forward to it!"

I smile at her once more before turning around and walking away. As I approach the chip aisle, I realize I haven't even told her my name. When I text her, it's going to be a random number that she won't recognize, and all I'll be able to introduce myself as is "the guy who ordered the steak and sausage from you earlier."

So, whirling back around, I clear my throat. She's helping another customer, then she looks at me and raises a questioning eyebrow.

"Forgot to tell you my name," I say with a sheepish look. "Aidan."

"Oh! Uh, nice to meet you, Aidan. You already know my name," she says, pointing to her tag and tapping her finger against it.

"Right. Text you later, Colleen," I say, feeling much calmer now that I've fixed that.

I finish my shopping a few minutes later and head home.

It's only when the quesadillas are finally cooking in the pan and I hear Dara's car pulling into the driveway that I send her a text,

Hey it's Aidan. Want to grab a coffee this weekend?

Hopefully, she'll answer when she gets off work. My brothers and I finish up dinner and clean the dishes. They're bitching about the shop and I can't even wrap my head around it. I'm too busy thinking about Colleen. I wonder what she's like at home. Probably a lot nicer and funnier than Ally. Cheating bitch. I hope I never see her again. Nowhere in Pythos. Not in my life. Or my dreams.

Damn! I can't go out with Colleen. Not with this much pent up frustration about Ally. I need to get over her, first.

Colleen deserves someone who can put his full attention on her, not someone still in the throes of heartbreak.

I wouldn't wish rebound sex on anyone, especially not a nice girl like her.

What was I thinking?

4

*C*olleen

I respond to Aidan's text the second I walk into my house. I may also have done a little happy dance because I'm excited. This is the first time since Asher and I broke up that I've felt hopeful about my romantic prospects.

Of course, thinking of Asher immediately puts a damper on my mood, but I shove thoughts of him aside and take off my shoes and walk to the fridge. Inside there are leftovers from a new spicy pasta recipe I tried, and I grab a fork from the drawer and start eating, not even bothering to heat it up.

Thoughts of Asher cross my mind again as I'm eating, since he always loved spicy food. It was one of the first things we bonded over when we were both getting our chef certificates. We'd finish class and then find some hole-in-the-wall place to stuff ourselves, and L.A. was great for that. There were always new restaurants and neighborhoods to explore.

He broke up with me because I wouldn't stay there with him, not after Grandma died and left me her house. He told me I should sell it and we could use the money to buy our own place in Hollywood, or somewhere equally cool. He hated the idea of moving to Pythos where there aren't any 5-star restaurants.

But I knew I'd end up here. I might have moved to L.A., hoping to spend the rest of my twenties there, but I knew I'd come back to Pythos, eventually. Grandma told me years ago she was leaving the house to me. Hopefully, I'll have a grandkid I can pass it on to someday and the tradition will continue.

My thoughts turn back to Aidan. I wonder how long he's lived in Pythos. I can't wait to have coffee with him. I have the weekend off, so if the date goes well and turns into dinner, and then a night of passionate lovemaking back at my place, I have the time. Not that I'm getting my hopes up or anything, but having a gorgeous man for the night sounds thrilling.

$\sim$

Annnnd…I do get my hopes up, which sucks, because three days later, he still hasn't responded to my text…

"Yes! Saturday, 3pm, at the café on Smith?"

Was I too forward?

I shouldn't even have time to think about all this with the amount of work I have. Between the early shifts at the store, blogging, and finishing up the recipe testing for the cookbook contest, I'm barely sleeping. Nearly every waking hour is occupied, and yet my brain still finds time to have a serious freak out about the possibility that I've screwed up my only chance with Pythos' hottest bachelor.

Things finally come to a head on Friday when Robert pulls me aside and tells me I almost served real beef to a customer who ordered the vegan burgers we sell. This is a serious faux pas, and he suggests I spend the rest of the day in the back where I can get a grip.

"Colleen, what's up with you? You're not usually this careless," Petey says from where he's standing in front of the fridge, arranging the cuts of meat.

"I just have a lot on my mind, that's all," I tell him. I want to expand on that, to spill all my woes, but while Petey is a great guy, he's not really who I would go to for romantic advice. I tried once, but he and his wife have been together for so long, he's completely forgotten the rest of us single people have to go through hell to try to find that special someone.

Instead, I throw myself into work, letting the repetitive sound of the slicer as it cuts and slices put my mind into a meditative state. It works, and the rest of my shift flies by. I'm in such a good mood that I don't even check my phone the minute I get to the locker room, as has been my habit for the last few days. Instead, I make the slow drive home, deciding to stop off at my favorite Thai place for their dinner special.

I don't look at my phone until I'm getting ready for bed hours later, which is how I almost miss the text from Aidan.

"Hey, sorry for the radio silence. Lost my phone for a few days. Turns out I left it in a customer's car! Anyway, would you mind moving coffee to next Saturday instead? My brother took off suddenly for a car show and I'm left doing all his detail work."

I breathe deeper than I have in days as I slide back onto my pillows, a silly grin taking over my face. He wasn't ghosting me. I wasn't too eager. It wasn't my fault at all!

I quickly type a reply, letting him know that next Saturday works fine, and that I'm glad he found his phone.

~

Over the next week, Aidan and I text nearly every day, about everything from our favorite food bloggers and Food Network shows to the best food and travel books we've read in the last year. He loves Anthony Bourdain as much as I do, which is good, because I can't date a man who doesn't appreciate the prowess of the late, great Tony.

I'm hesitant at first to tell him about my blog. The only other guy I've been on a date with this year took one look at it and asked why I was wasting my time writing it when food blogging has become so passé.

"It's such a saturated field. Maybe you should just switch it to Instagram. That seems to be the best platform these days," he'd told me on our third and final date.

But when I mention it to Aidan, he's so excited he uses three emojis and more exclamation points than your average thirty-something-year-old man should, which makes him even more adorable. He even tries out a few of my recipes, making my favorite Pad Thai, and even my grandma's chilaquiles. He sends me pictures of the finished dishes and says that Grandma's chilaquiles are better than any he's ever tried.

Aidan tells me he loves Cali-Mexican food, so I suggest that, instead of meeting for coffee this weekend, we meet for lunch. He readily agrees, and I suggest we meet at Chalupas at 2pm on Saturday. Two days away. Two days until I get to see him again!

～

Friday after work, I open my locker and fish my phone out of my bag. No texts. I send Aidan a quick hello, how are you message, and check that we're still on for the next day.

Hours go by, during the time I drive home, make myself dinner, test two more recipes while I'm at it, and clean my kitchen. I avoid looking at my phone the entire time, waiting until I've put the vacuum back in the closet, then take the phone off the charger.

And just like that, all my smiles and pleasant mood from the past week fly out the window, replaced by a growing sense of dread. He's ghosting me. Wonderful Aidan who loves cooking, Anthony Bourdain, and who seems so perfect for me is a ghost.

A part of me hopes he's just busy, but when I check my phone again, he hasn't responded. Our date must be cancelled, my mood is crappy, I have a cookbook to finish, and no desire to do anything.

5

*a*idan
  Thank God it's Friday. It's been a shitty week.

I don't remember leaving my phone sitting on the tool chest in the corner of the shop. A tool chest I haven't used in at least a month, but there it sits.

I thought I'd lost my phone over a week ago, and honestly, I didn't care. The only thing I use it for is to text my brothers anyway, and considering I see them every day, it's not a big deal.

I even thought I might not replace it. I'd save myself the humiliation of texting girls I shouldn't be with and avoid Brodie's stupid videos altogether. Win-win situation.

I stare at the phone, but no matter how long I look at the messages, I can't make sense of what's going on.

I'm surprised it still has any battery left, but as I scroll through the texts, I notice something weird. Emojis. I never use them, and honestly, I find them annoying. I don't want to have to search through a thousand little cartoon faces to find a picture that adequately expresses how I'm feeling. It's stupid and a total waste of time.

But Dara loves to use them. I scroll through the texts again, and I realize what he's done. I'm disgusted to read and re-read that he's asked Colleen out on a date on my behalf...for tomorrow!

What the fuck?

Is he planning to impersonate me on this date? We might be brothers, but Dara and I don't look remotely enough alike for her to mistake him for me. I'm confused and getting angrier by the second as I stomp through the door of Dara's workshop. My brothers are clustered around the counter, digging into the burgers Dara picked up for our lunch.

"Hey! Got your double bacon with extra pickles and extra-large fries, though you better eat them quick before Mr. Piggy eats them all," Dara says, gesturing at Brodie.

"Fuck the fries. What the fuck have you been doing with my phone? Did you send these texts?" I ask, storming toward him and picking up a bag of screws that I throw at his head. He ducks and catches them with one hand, his other still holding his burger.

As he lowers his hand, I see his face and the expression on it is a mix of guilt and amusement. He looks pleased with himself. That makes me want to deck him. I clench my fist at my side, but wait for him to speak, giving him a chance to explain himself.

"Before you freak out on me, let me explain," Dara says, putting down his burger and holding his hands up in defense.

"Fine," I bark out. "Go ahead."

"We have the same phone and I accidentally took yours instead of mine to a visit at the high school last week when they called me over to fix their SmartBoard. I didn't realize it was yours until it buzzed, and I saw a notification from a girl named Colleen."

"Okay...and?" I say, waiting for him to get to the meat and potatoes. So far nothing he's said is making me any less angry.

"When I realized it was your phone, I swear I was going to give it back to you, but when I got back to the shop, I recognized the name and number. They looked familiar, so I checked my database and saw it was Colleen Mathers, the cute girl from the grocery store. She brought her coffeemaker in here a week or so ago to get fixed."

"So fucking what?" I say, angrily, then he takes a bite of his burger and continues.

"She's perfect for you, Aidan," he says, with a mouth full of burger. "She's into food, she's friendly, and she's fucking hot. I've talked to her a few times at the meat counter and when she brought her coffeemaker in here, I just thought it was crazy of you to ignore her without even giving things a chance. I mean, you've been alone for a while now, and I know Ally hurt you bad, but—"

"But, what? You fucking impersonated me? You texted her, pretending to be me?" I interrupt, and I'm seething inside.

"Yeah. I was going to show you the texts today and convince you to go on the date with her tomorrow. I put your phone back on that tool chest so you'd find it. Connor and Brodie were in on it, too," Dara says, shooting our brothers beseeching looks, hoping for support.

"It's true," Connor says. "You need to get back out there again, Aidan. Sitting at home, burying your sorrow in books and Mom's quesadillas isn't going to help you. We want you to be happy... like me and Alana, and I know you're capable of that. You were happy before. Be happy again, 'cause, bro, I'm tired of the grumpy ass bastard you've become."

"I second that. I know deception isn't the best way to start a relationship, but we had to do something. We're worried about you, dude. If you don't start dating again and get some positive romantic experiences under your belt, you're going to stay grumpy and single forever," Brodie says, scratching the back of his neck.

It makes me feel a little better. At least he copped to what he did. Connor and Dara, however, look perfectly satisfied with themselves; like they don't care at all that they've been meddling, not only in my life, but Colleen's as well. They don't realize they're setting her up for rejection and disappointment that she doesn't deserve.

"In case any of you have forgotten, I'm a grown man," I say. "I can make my own decisions about my love life, and if I decide I don't want to date a girl, I don't need any of my nosy brothers trying to convince me otherwise."

I step forward, grab the food bag marked *Aidan* and stalk out of the room. I'll eat my burger in Connor's office where it's quiet and none of these idiots will bother me. There's no way I'm going on a date with Colleen tomorrow. I'm not the happy-go-lucky, emoji and exclamation point kind of guy in those texts.

Dara may have gotten my favorite food blogs, cooking shows, and chefs right, but he didn't get the real me down in those texts. I'm a jaded, grumpy bastard who's perfectly content to spend the rest of his life alone.

I'm not going on that date with her at all. The guy she's expecting isn't the one who'll show up. Dara has crafted a much better version of me in those texts, but the original doesn't compare.

I don't want to see Colleen's beautiful face fall into a frown when she realizes she's stuck on a date with the real me. No way in hell will I let that happen.

6

*C*olleen

The date didn't happen... obviously. I had a secret hope that I'd wake up on Saturday morning to a text from Aidan explaining his silence, but when none came, I wasn't surprised. It was too good to be true. I should've known that from the start. I've never dated anyone that similar to me, or that gorgeous before. It was a pipe dream, plain and simple.

Thankfully, the cookbook proposal is due the Monday after what would have been our date, and I'm so busy putting the finishing touches on my submission that I barely have time to think about him...*much*.

I'll admit he enters my thoughts now and again, but I've saved testing the bread recipes until last, so I can take out my frustration on the dough. I knead it fiercely while I make several loaves. The best is the focaccia recipe, which requires me to throw the dough onto the counter.

I imagine it's Aidan's head I'm throwing the dough at. His stupidly gorgeous face getting smacked repeatedly with a gooey mixture of flour, water and yeast. It helps.

~

I still went to Chalupas by myself on Saturday and ate chilaquiles. The combination of soft tortilla, runny fried egg, and spicy salsa was a perfect balm for my heartache. I've been eating them non-stop ever since, reciting Grandma's recipe as I crumble the soft cheese onto the dish. Her voice in my head is so soothing, and I miss her more this week than I have in a long time.

If she were here, she'd tell me everything would be okay. She'd tell me I come from a powerful line of women who were the backbone of their families. She'd tell me that female strength is in my DNA, and that I can get through anything. Whenever she said it, I'd always believed her but now, reciting it to myself, it sounds totally fucking stupid.

I dedicate the cookbook to her, and I'm crying as I send the submission just before midnight. The tears are a mixture of relief, sadness, loss, and rejection. I want someone to celebrate this milestone with me, but I'm all alone.

Thankfully, I wake up the next morning feeling a little less sappy. Robert and Petey take me out to lunch to celebrate sending in the cookbook, and I meet some of my yoga friends after work for cocktails.

Everything goes well until Thursday afternoon when I want to go to the store and discover my car won't start, and it isn't the first time. It's an old 1995 Toyota Camry that can be temperamental at the best of times, and after over an hour of trying to get her to start, I realize it's time to call an auto repair shop.

Dara McKinley mentioned that his brothers did auto repairs, and he'd give me a discount next time I came in, since the coffeemaker took longer to fix than he planned. I call over there and a nice, deep-voiced guy answers and tells me he'll send someone right over to look at the car.

I sit back in my seat feeling a little less stressed, since I figure if Dara's brothers are as good with cars as he is with my coffeemaker, then the car will be fine.

Fifteen minutes later a truck pulls up next to me, and a man steps out. I only see his torso from my vantage point in the driver's seat, but I swear I'd recognize those pecs and biceps anywhere.

Oh. My. God. It's Aidan.

He knocks on the roof of my car and when I open the door; I try to paste on an innocent smile for him as I get out. I must fail though, because no sooner do his eyes meet mine, he's openly staring back at me. His mouth moves like he's trying to speak, but he doesn't quite know what to say.

I'm in the same boat, standing there looking at him like I've seen a ghost, or in this case, the man who ghosted me.

"Colleen," he finally spits out.

"Hi, Aidan," I say, raising my hand for the world's most awkward wave.

"Is this your car?" he asks, pointing past me to the vehicle I just stepped out of.

I raise an eyebrow, thinking it's a kinder way of saying "Yeah, duh!"

"What seems to be the problem?" he asks, moving away from me and around to the hood.

"I don't know. I got in and tried to start her up, but nothing happens. Just an awful screeching sound every time I turn the key," I explain as I duck my head back into the car and pull the lever to pop the hood.

When I look back up, he's already lifted the hood and I'm treated to the sight of Aidan's magnificent ass as he bends over the left side of the car, checking something under there. I move a little closer behind him, but all I can see is his scruffy jawline, his long, tanned neck, and those shoulders. Shoulders that lead to the best pair of arms in the world; his muscles twitching and flexing as he fiddles with something in the engine.

After a few minutes, he stands up and heads toward his work truck in silence. He comes back with a toolbox, which he sets on the ground. I watch him as he goes back to work on the car and there's a sound of metal clinking on metal, then he gets out from under the hood and comes toward me.

I step out of the way, tripping on a hole in the asphalt and stumbling, but he catches me. One muscular hand comes to the small of my back, and his other to my hip as he draws me back up straight again. A look of searing hot need passes between us, and I wonder if he's going to kiss me, but he immediately drops his hand and leans inside the car, turning the key in the ignition. The screeching sound starts again, and his shoulders hunch. I imagine his brow furrowing as he tries to figure out what's wrong.

I can still feel the warmth of his hands on me fifteen minutes later when he finally fixes whatever was wrong with the car. The heat from his fingers has left warm patches on my skin, and though I know I'm exaggerating, I can't help but wonder if I'll find the outline of his hands on my body when I go to take a shower.

I feel a tingle between my legs and my mind races with that thought. I imagine Aidan joining me in it, soaping his hands up before rubbing them up and down my body, making me feel both deliciously clean and sinfully dirty at the same time.

I imagine him dropping to his knees, spreading my legs, and burying his head between them.

"Uh, Colleen? Are you okay?" I look up to find he's been speaking to me for God knows how long.

"Sorry! I was thinking about um... my... uh cookbook!" I lie.

"Right, of course," he nods, avoiding my eyes as he switches his toolbox from one hand to the other.

"So, is she all fixed?" I ask, nodding toward the car.

"Yup. It was just a loose belt. Easily fixed," he says, running a hand through his hair. I notice he has little freckles dotting his hairline, and I have the strangest urge to reach up on my tiptoes and kiss them.

I refrain since that would be uncalled for and weird, but the urge to touch him remains. Even with how angry I am at him for how he treated me, I still want him. He's impossible to resist.

"Do I owe you anything?" I ask, trying to distract myself.

"Nope!" he says, a little more aggressively than necessary.

I raise my eyebrows in surprise, and he explains. "It's the least I could do. After…you know…"

"After you fucking stood me up?" I say, not caring how bitter it comes out.

"Yeah. Look, I'm really sorry about that," he says, shoving his hand in his pocket. He looks so uncomfortable. I almost feel bad for him. Almost.

"Whatever, Aidan. If you didn't want to go out with me, you could have just told me. I'm a big girl. I can handle rejection, but I have a hard time handling guys who string me along and then suddenly ghost me the day before a date. It's hurtful and disrespectful."

I glare at him, and when his eyes finally rise to meet mine, I see he's struggling with something. He doesn't just look contrite or guilty. He looks…*sad*? Confused? Angry? I'm not sure. I don't know him well enough to tell. He didn't give me the chance to get to know him well enough.

"I didn't reject you. Or at least, I didn't mean to," he

says, setting the toolbox down. "Colleen, it's not what you think. Please, let me explain."

I cross my arms, both wanting to hear what he has to say, and knowing that whatever excuse he gives me won't be enough. But because I'm a sucker for a sob story, I say, "Go ahead. Explain."

*a*idan

"I had every intention of going on a date with you, Colleen. I mean, you're beautiful, you're smart, and you're a foodie. You're basically my dream girl." It sounds lame coming out of my mouth and I worry she'll think I'm bullshitting her, but when I look up, I see a slight smile flash across her face. Encouraged, I continue.

"I wanted to go on a date with you, but after I texted you, I got caught up in this flashback of hurt and emotions and... well, I wasn't exactly in the right state of mind." I feel myself getting riled up just talking about it so I take a deep breath before I continue. Colleen, saint that she is, waits patiently with no discernible emotion on her face.

"I broke up with my ex-girlfriend a few months ago and it was bad. Terrible. She'd cheated on me and one day, I walked in on her and a friend of mine having sex on the couch we'd just bought together a few weeks before." Colleen winces, and her face melts into a sympathetic expression.

"That's awful. I'm so sorry, Aidan," she says, and I can tell she really means it.

"Thanks, yeah, it was. We'd been dating for three years, moved in together, and I thought she was the girl I was going to spend the rest of my life with. Being rejected like that was... well, it kind of fucked up my head. A lot," I say, shaking my head.

She gives me an understanding nod, gesturing for me to continue.

"I've always been an introvert, but these last few months I've turned into a loner. I go to the shop, the gym, then I go home. I talk as little as I can get away with and spend most of my free time by myself. I haven't dated anyone. Hell, I haven't even really talked to a girl until you. I'm..."

"Afraid to let anyone else in? In case they hurt you again?" she fills in like she's reading my mind.

"Exactly," I say. She seems to know me so well and we've barely spoken. Has Dara's impersonation of me via text messages been accurate enough that she has a clear picture of me in her mind? I don't know whether to be happy or angered by that but, either way, I like being understood, especially from a woman as sexy as Colleen.

"I know how you feel because I'm in the same situation. My boyfriend broke up with me when I moved back here last year. It devastated me. We met at chef school and I thought we were destined to be together as well," Colleen tells me, nervously shoving a lock of hair behind her ear.

A spark of jealousy flies through me at the mention of her ex, but I try to ignore it. I can't let my emotions get the better of me. I want to listen to her. Whatever she has to say is important, and besides, what right do I have to be jealous, when I'm not even her boyfriend? As of right now, I'm nothing to her, thanks to my own asinine antics.

"My grandma died and left me her house. I grew up visiting her here every summer, and I always wanted to come back. Pythos is my home. But he didn't understand. He didn't get how I could choose some podunk desert town over a city like L.A., with all its opportunities," she says, rolling her eyes. "I've just thrown myself into my work since we broke up. I got the house set up, got a job at the store, and spend almost all my free time working on my food blog. Oh, and a cookbook contest I'm trying to win and get it published. I thought they'd be enough to make me happy, but they aren't. They can't make up for human interaction, or intimacy," she says, her cheeks flushing at that last word.

I'm feeling heat, too, but not in my cheeks. It's much lower than that, and I move to adjust my pants.

"Yeah, I hear ya. On one hand, I'm afraid of getting hurt again, on the other, I want to get back to normal, whatever that is. After I felt a connection to you at the grocery store, all those feelings of anger and resentment about my ex resurfaced. So I just figured I wasn't ready to date again. Especially not with you," I say.

Colleen frowns, and when I realize the implication of my words, I add, "What I mean is, you deserve someone who's devoted to you. Someone who focuses all their attention on you and doesn't have any emotional baggage distracting them."

She softens, a smile appearing on her lips, but she shakes her head at me. "Aidan, that's silly. Everyone has emotional baggage. It comes with the territory of being an adult. I would've liked you, despite your emotional scars, as long as you accepted mine."

"Would have?" I ask, hating that she's using past tense.

"Well, it's not like you gave me the opportunity to get to know you. You texted me non-stop for a week, then suddenly ghosted me. You didn't even give me a chance," she says, with a hint of sadness.

And now comes the part where I have to explain that she hasn't been texting me, she's been texting Dara. Awkward. I suck in a deep breath and steel myself. I have to be honest with her. If anything's going to happen between us, it has to start on a foundation of truth.

"See, the thing is, it wasn't me who texted you. It was my younger brother, Dara," I say, but I can't get any more words out before Colleen's eyes widen and she yells at me, so loud it makes the birds perched in the nearby tree fly away.

"WHAT!?"

"Hold on!" I hold up my hand in surrender and talk

quickly, hardly taking a breath between sentences. "Let me explain. Dara accidentally took my phone the day after I texted you. So when you texted me back, he saw it. He realized I was chickening out of going out with you, so he impersonated me. He planned to tell me on Friday, to convince me to go out with you, but I found my phone before he told me."

"So, what did you do when you found your phone?" she yells, and I can't help thinking how fucking sexy she looks when she's angry.

"Well, I read through the texts, confronted Dara, and he confessed. He said I should still go on the date with you, but I was so pissed off at him, Colleen," I say, hoping she'll understand. From the look on her face, I don't think she does. She probably thinks I'm an idiot. "I know it's a pathetic excuse, but I'm a very private person. I'm the oldest of my family, and to have Dara meddling in my business is embarrassing. I hope you can understand that. Realizing he could do such a passable impersonation of me via text just felt so intrusive and humiliating."

"Not as humiliating as getting stood up on a date I'd spent a week looking forward to," Colleen counters. "My first date in over a year," she adds, driving the knife in deeper.

"Ouch," I concede. "I'm really sorry. I've been a total asshole, but I want to make it up to you. I like you, Colleen…a lot. And while your impression of me is from texts sent by my brother, everything he said about me is true. I love Anthony Bourdain and the Food Network. I spent all last night reading your blog and made all the recipes Dara said I had, and your chocolate cake is so good, I could eat it every day."

She laughs, which I take as a good sign. Maybe some of her anger is melting away.

"Please, let me take you out. Let me take you to dinner at Chalupas. We can order the entire menu and enjoy the spicy food and you can spend the whole evening telling me what a jackass I've been."

"Fine," she says, and I nearly whoop for joy, but then she adds a caveat. "But we aren't going to Chalupas. I've eaten a lot of chilaquiles this week. They're my go-to comfort food."

"Patricio's, then?" I suggest, naming the small Italian place near the high school with the checkered tablecloths and sinfully good *arrabbiatta* sauce.

"Okay," she says, opening her car door. "But one wrong move and it's over. You'll never be welcome in the meat department again," she says teasingly.

"I'll pick you up at seven?"

"I can't wait," she says, and drives off with a wave out the window.

I practically skip back to my car and pat myself on the back, then rush home to get cleaned up, even though I still have a few hours before our date.

There's no way I'm taking my dream girl out in grease-stained jeans. Colleen deserves only the best and from now on, that's exactly what I'm going to give her.

8

*C*olleen

Tonight is my tenth date with Aidan. It's been a little over four weeks since he apologized and took me out for the best dinner ever, which also happened to be the night of our first kiss.

Now, I'm finally confident he isn't going to run out on me. We've gotten to know each other on a deeper level. We talk all the time and share our hopes, our fears, our childhoods, and I'm comfortable around him. He makes me feel like I can be myself.

I'm also a ball of raging lady hormones that's about to explode any second. So far, we've avoided taking things to the bedroom. But he's built... everywhere. Arms, chest, legs, and... *cock*. I've felt it long and thick, pressing up against me through our clothes more than once while we kissed.

I've been dreaming about this. I want to have sex with him. Tonight. Not because I know it'll be amazing, but because I can't concentrate anymore. Thoughts of him fucking me make it hard to focus on anything, work, blogging, cooking. Even brushing my teeth gives me the shivers.

Thanks to my wickedly dirty thoughts of Aidan, I've burned two loaves of bread this week and nearly put salt in a cake, rather than sugar. The situation needs rectifying, and I have a sneaking suspicion he'll be more than happy with my solution.

I have it all planned out, too. I'm making chilaquiles. The tortillas are hot and ready; the cheese is grated, and the fresh salsa is ready to go.

I've bathed, shaved, powdered all my sexy bits and selected my power outfit. A little black dress I bought at a vintage shop years ago. It hugs my curves in all the right places and dips down just low enough that the red lace bralette I'm wearing is on show.

I've also made Mexican chocolate cake and I'm going to whip up some Margaritas. I'm excited, if not a little nervous, but tequila always calms me down. And I want everything to be perfect.

I barely finish pouring the cocktails into salt-rimmed glasses when there's a knock at the front door. I practically leap into the entryway and have to stop myself from throwing the door open and taking Aidan into my arms. Instead, I let my excitement show in my smile as I take his hand and pull him inside.

"Hey there," I say, planting a soft kiss on his lips.

"Hey, yourself. You look beautiful, Colleen," His eyes travel from my face down to my chest then lower, all the way to my freshly painted red toenails.

"Thanks," I say, beaming, and lead him into the kitchen. "Dinner should be ready in a few minutes. I'm almost finished with the eggs and I have fresh chips and guacamole, too."

"You are the perfect woman," he says. I know he's joking, but I feel a warm tingling between my legs. I'm so excited because I know tonight is the night. If I can hold on until after dinner.

Aidan loves the food! I'm so horny and nervous and growing more so during the meal. And to top it off, the butterflies in my stomach are making it hard for me to focus. I was so excited earlier, but now I'm terrified that the next part of our evening will crash and burn. After all, it's been over a year since I've had sex. Over a year since I was naked in front of a man who wasn't my gyno. What if I can't satisfy him? Or, what if Aidan doesn't like what's underneath my little black dress?

He must sense my internal turmoil, because he reaches his hand out to take mine and squeezes gently.

"Everything okay?" he asks. "You look a little freaked out."

"No!" I say, but my voice cracks as I reply and there's a terrible silence that follows as my voice echoes around the room. I wince and say, "No," again, this time at normal volume and tone.

"Come here," he says, and tugs my hand. I stand and walk around the table to him, then Aidan pulls me down onto his lap. "Tell me what's on your mind, Colleen. Come on, we said we'd be honest with each other no matter what."

I straddle his hips and close my eyes, embarrassed. "I really want to have sex with you, but I'm afraid I won't satisfy you. Or, maybe you'll think I'm gross underneath this dress, and then you won't like me anymore." God, just saying it makes me sound like a whiny bitch.

I keep my eyes closed after I finish, afraid of what he might say, but when a few seconds pass with no reaction from him, curiosity gets the best of me and I peek out of one eye.

Aidan's looking at me with what I can only describe as a goofy, lovesick face. He looks like one of the dogs in Lady and the Tramp in the scene where they share the spaghetti. It's a funny look on such an outrageously handsome man, and I'm about to tell him, but then he leans in and kisses me. It's a whisper of a kiss, his lips just barely brushing against mine, but it's enough to make me feel like my knees are made of jello.

"It's you and me. How can it be anything other than spectacular?" he says, brushing against my lips again. His breaths alternately cool and warm my mouth, sending shivers all over me.

I smile and lean in, sliding my hands up his chest to his neck. I pull him toward me, crushing our mouths together. I forget the cake sitting on the counter, and the half-finished cocktails on the table.

They aren't nearly as delicious as what's about to happen next.

9

*A*idan
  I'm glad Colleen told me how nervous she is. I'm confident about my bedroom skills, but being with someone new is nerve-wracking, and that's without adding in the entire shifter thing.

I don't shift often, but we all have our triggers. It can happen to me when I'm nervous. Thankfully, I live a fairly predictable life, so there aren't many situations that cause it. Having sex with the woman of my dreams, however, is definitely one such situation.

I keep my cool as Colleen and I kiss at her kitchen table. For a while, I lose myself in the feel of her soft skin beneath my fingertips. I slide the silk straps of her dress off her shoulders, allowing me a better view of the sexy lace bra she's wearing.

And damn, is she sexy.

Her breasts spill over the tiny triangular scraps of

lace. I can barely see the outline of her nipples through the fabric and I lick my lips, aching to suck one of those sweet little nubs into my mouth. I lean in and place my mouth over the lace. Colleen gasps and tilts her head back. She pushes her chest out further and I welcome her, wrapping my arms around her back and pulling her closer to me.

She smells like flowers and woman, a combination that has my head swimming as I tease her nipple with my tongue, licking and sucking it and swirling my tongue around. I'm more relaxed, but my cock grows harder with every passing second, making my boxer briefs uncomfortably tight. It doesn't help that Colleen is grinding on my lap, but there's no way in hell I'm going to ask her to stop. It feels too good.

It's only when I'm carrying her to her room that my nervousness reappears.

Fuck. Me.

The sight of her bed is what sparks me off. It's so neatly made, with a lilac comforter turned down and candles in ornate lanterns on the bedside table. My skin prickles, sending shivers down my back.

"Aidan? You okay?" Colleen asks when I set her down on the bed and step back, shoving my hands into my pockets.

"Yeah, of course. Totally fine," I say with a conviction I don't feel. I'm nodding my head, but I can tell she doesn't believe me. She raises an eyebrow, then reaches out her hand, beckoning me toward her.

"Come here," she says. I try to relax, rolling my shoulders back and focusing on the gorgeous woman in front of me. I have to stay cool, calm, and human. I take her hand and kneel in front of her, trying to will my body to stay calm. Which is a huge feat since my dick is hard as a rock.

It works for a few seconds as I help her out of her dress and slowly untie the bows on the sides of her bra and panties, making them even more fun to remove. The sight of her takes my breath away. In the candlelight, she looks radiant. A goddess with golden skin and hair that falls in waves over her shoulders and tumbles over her breasts.

"Damn, Colleen. You're the most beautiful woman I've ever seen," I say, my voice thick with desire and I mean every word. I could spend all night just staring at her if my cock would stop throbbing in my pants. I draw her closer, leaning down to kiss her legs, her belly, and her hips.

"Mmm, that feels good. Come lay with me," she says, patting the bed beside her.

I tear off my shirt, and Colleen giggles as I drop my boxers along with my jeans and my hard cock springs free. As soon as I'm naked, I push her back onto the sheets and launch myself on top of her. We bounce, and she giggles again. God, I could listen to that sound for the rest of my life. I love it…and I love her.

Did I really just think that? Yes, I love her!

The words repeat in my mind as we kiss. She curls

her fingers around my cock and slides her hand up and down, increasing my need for release. I never thought I'd fall in love again, but while Colleen murmurs sexily wicked things in my ear of what she wants to do with me, I realize how much I want her, *need* her.

I move my body so I can caress her stomach, my hand sliding down to her wet lips. And, oh God, is she wet! My cock twitches, wanting to be inside her, and at the moment—this very fucking moment—it all becomes too much, and I feel myself shifting into a goddamn cobra!

Fuck!

God help me! This can't be happening!

I'm so fucked.

Biological snakes have two dicks that are usually inverted inside their body, except during mating. And, right now, my fucking cobra thinks it's mating!

When my cock divides into two, it's an embarrassing humiliation to what's becoming the new all-time low of my life. I brace myself for Colleen's look of disgust, and to see her running, screaming, out of the room. I coil into the bed, slowly turning my eyes to her. She's totally calm and smiling.

"Oh, Aidan. Are you a shifter, too?"

10

*C*olleen

"It's okay," I tell Aidan the cobra, scooting closer to him all coiled up. It's hard to tell what a six-foot cobra is thinking or feeling, but I think I can still talk some sense into him, even in his shifted form. I don't even know if he understands me. But I can try.

I know shifters need to feel non-threatened, so I continue talking to him in a calming voice until he finally uncoils and shifts back to human form. He looks around in surprise for a moment, then his eyes are on me.

"Colleen. Fuck! I am so sorry. I—" he says and jumps up off of the bed.

I hold up my hand. "No! Stop! You don't have to apologize. I get it. It's part of your nature. My mom was a wolf shifter, and she shifted when she got scared or angry, so I'm used to being around shifters."

"Really?" He still looks surprised, though somewhat

more relieved as his cobra hood relaxes back into him and the worry leaves his face.

I nod. "Yeah. She died when I was in high school. An anti-shifter gang murdered her, and everyone else in my family are shifters. I'm the only one whose genes didn't manifest into one. Well, not yet, anyway."

"Wow. I'm sorry about your mom. That's awful," Aidan says and sits back down on the bed next to me.

"It's okay. It was a long time ago, and honestly, we had a pretty hard relationship. She was a very volatile person. I was going to tell you about her, eventually, but she's… it's hard to talk about her. Painful still" I explain.

"I know what you mean. My relationship with my parents was good when they were alive, but it's complicated now that they're gone."

"Were they shifters?" I ask, leaning back into the pillows and patting the spot next to me. Aidan slides up beside me, then we both turn toward each other at the same time and Aidan's cock is right there. Front and center. Begging to be touched.

"Yeah, they were, but I really don't want to talk about that right now. I wanna talk about this," he says, and snakes his arm around my waist, pulling me closer.

"So, two cocks? Is that a snakey cobra-type thing?" I ask him, thinking how amazing it would feel to have two cocks inside me at the same time.

He chuckles, "Yes, and no. In Cobra form if my cobra is around for mating season, yes. In human form, you only get one. Sorry," he says, with a crooked grin.

My hand inches down his belly to his cock and I whisper, "Not sorry at all." I dip my head lower, taking the tip in my mouth. The hiss he lets out makes my pussy ache even more and I stroke and suck, reveling in the taste of him.

Aidan must enjoy it because he coils his fingers in my hair and slides his cock deeper down my throat. My body hums with need and I pull back with a 'pop'.

"Come here, fuck me. I've waited so long for this," I tell him, and lay back on the bed. He's on top of me in a split second, his fingers toying with my clit.

Aidan lets out a groan as he slips inside me. I'm so wet, there's no hesitation. "Yes! Like that!" I cry out when he pushes into me. He hits THAT spot with ease and I can feel an orgasm already building.

Aidan is a lot taller than I am and he takes both of my hands into one of his and raises it above my head. I'm powerless except for my hips and it feels amazing.

"You like that?" he asks, and I can only nod. My legs fly up and curl around his ass, my heels pulling him in deeper.

"Yes, I'm gonna come! Fuck yes, right there!" My entire body vibrates as his other hand grabs my hip and he holds me there, pounding into me in a steady rhythm. Stars flash behind my eyes. This is it.

"Aidan! Come with me! Come on!" I cry out as the rush of the best orgasm I've ever had flows through me. His face scrunches up and the most magnificent thing happens. His hood expands a little and he shivers and shudders, letting out a hiss that shakes the entire house. His hot come shoots into me with a heat that sets my soul on fire.

Oh God, is he marking me? Is this what mating feels like to the shifter world?

"Fuuuuck, Colleen. Fuck," he cries out on a groan and falls to the side. I'm in heaven. Or what I think heaven should be.

"Aidan?" I say, with a hot sigh. I'm still trying to catch my breath, but Aidan seems to be calmer than he should be.

"Yeah?" he asks, raising an eyebrow.

"Did you fucking mark me?" I ask.

"Mark you? How?" He seems puzzled.

I turn on my elbow and look into his eyes, but he's looking at the ceiling. "When you came, I felt it. Hot, and it hit my insides all the way down to my soul. My veins were on fire. Is that what happens with shifters?"

Aidan's gaze moves to mine, his eyes are black, but not scary. "I don't know, Colleen. I felt it too. I've never felt it before. You have to realize this is all new to me."

"I love you, Aidan" I say, and the words feel so right, like the most honest thing I've ever said.

He breaks out into the widest smile I've ever seen. He reaches over, placing a hand on my cheek, and says, "I love you, too, Colleen. Wanna see if we can get that feeling again?"

"Yes, yes, I do!" I say and slide my leg across him. This time, I will be the one in control.

11

*A*idan

Colleen smiles; sultry and sinful. I've never felt this way. Ever.

"Do you want it slow, or fast?" she asks as she straddles my hips and places her pussy right on the head of my cock.

"Slow. Let's take it slow," I say, then she slides her pussy down on me and the heat she emanates makes my cock even harder. I've never been able to go two rounds so quickly. Colleen does something to me.

Something I want *more* of.

She grinds her pussy on me, slowly at first and her nipples peak in anticipation. I reach up and tweak one of the pretty pink things between my thumb and forefinger and when I do, Colleen shivers and moans.

I can tell she's almost there, and I want her to come, but I want to wait it out. I grab her hips in both hands and thrust into her, grinding the base of my cock on her clit. Then I recall what she asked me about two dicks and I trail my hand around her ass cheek and slide a slicked up finger inside her tight asshole.

"Oh fuck, Aidan," she bellows, and her orgasm comes fast and hard while I fill her two holes. Her ass fucks my finger as she grinds on my dick and I can't take it anymore. Within seconds, I'm so close to orgasm I can barely breathe.

"Faster, baby," I growl, and Colleen, being the perfect lover she is, quickens her pace, grinding my dick and fucking my finger until we both explode into one big delicious orgasm.

My hips buck hard against her, and my legs shake uncontrollably as wave after wave of delicious pleasure courses through my body and out my dick. Her pussy tightens around my cock and I throb and hiss as we reach our climax. Colleen is practically crying as she comes before we finally collapse together onto the bed.

I love feeling her weight on top of me as I trace kisses over her shoulders and breasts.

"Marry me, Colleen." I whisper into her neck.

Where'd that come from?

"Yes, Aidan. I'll marry you," she says without one iota of hesitation. My heart leaps into my throat knowing I've found my mate for life. After all the bullshit I've put us through, I never want to lose her. We can figure out the details later.

EPILOGUE

*C*olleen
Six Months Later

Life is so sweet when I wake up in Aidan's arms his hand caresses my pregnant belly. Once we found out I was pregnant, we had a quick wedding at the courthouse. Just me, Aidan and his three brothers.

We moved him into Grandma's house that night.

Living with a cobra shifter has its moments. For one, he likes to go out with his brothers to hunt. What? Bugs? Lizards? It's kind of icky, but my mom did it too, so I get it. And I love to watch him when his animal instincts kick in. I can't wait to see him be a father.

That also prompted the conversation about our gene pool. He's got were-dragon and cobra. I've got were-wolf, for sure, and I don't know if my father has any were-genes in him. The babies could be a lot of things, who knows? But one thing I do know is the babies will be loved and cared for no matter what genes they have.

My phone dings and it's an email informing me I've won the cookbook contest. "Colleen's Culinary Creations" will be published next Christmas, and the publisher wants to send me the prize money and will foot the bill for printing, publishing and everything.

"Aidan! Aidan!" I shake him awake. "I won the cookbook contest!"

He opens his eyes and smiles. "Great job!" he says and pulls me in closer to him. He smells so good. Even in the morning.

"Do you know what this means? It's a ten thousand dollar prize and they will publish it and sell it and everything! We're gonna be rich!" I exclaim. "I won't have to work for that bitch anymore. Now aren't you glad you married me?"

Aidan sits up against the headboard and looks at me, beaming. "Colleen, I love you. Cookbook or no cookbook. You are everything I've ever wanted in a wife and I didn't even know what that was before I met you."

Tears well in my eyes. I'm not sad, I'm happy. Or hormonal. "Oh my God, Aidan. I am so happy to have found you, cobra, and all. I can't wait to have these babies and love them—"

His eyes widen. "Babies?" he interrupts. "We're having babies? As in more than one?"

"Uh…yeah. What did you expect? I mean, your

brothers are twins, ya know." I say, not sure if he's okay with having an instant family.

Aidan jumps up off the bed and yells, "Fuck yeah!" a few times while he dances around the room. He pounds his chest with his fists like Tarzan.

This is it. What I've been praying for.

Aidan is happier, and more serene than I've ever seen him.

I'm happier too. Happy my cookbook won, and happy because I've found someone who loves me for who I am. Daughter of shifters, unabashed homebody, chef and lover of spicy chilaquiles and margaritas.

Aidan knows it and loves it all. And I feel the same way about him.

What more could a girl want?

THE END

ABOUT THE AUTHOR

Tilly Pope writes dirty, hot and over the top instalove stories about possessive alpha males who know what they want. Always short, sometimes cheesy, always naughty, no cheating and a guaranteed happily ever after.

Tilly loves football, spanking and wine.

Find her at tillypope.com

facebook.com/authortillypope

instagram.com/authortillypope

amazon.com/author/tillypope

Made in the USA
Las Vegas, NV
18 February 2025